WALT DISNEY'S

SAVAGE SAM

Based on the novel *"Savage Sam,"* by Fred Gipson,
published by Harper and Row. Told by Carl Memling.

Illustrated by Hamilton Greene

GOLDEN PRESS NEW YORK

THIS IS A BRAND-NEW BOOK, WRITTEN AND ILLUSTRATED
ESPECIALLY FOR GOLDEN BOOKS

Sam was a dog—a flop-eared, short-tailed, pot-bellied, happy, rascally dog. When it came to tackling food, he was savage. So they called him Savage Sam.

Arliss Coates was a boy—a round-faced, snub-nosed, freckled, happy, rascally boy. When it came to size, he was a short one. So they called him Little Arliss.

They lived in an old, log cabin farmhouse near Salt Licks, Texas.

Those two—Arliss Coates and Savage Sam—
did just about everything together.
They scattered the chickens together.

They **rode** Jumper the mule together.

And they hunted!

Sam ran through the woods, winding here and there, sniffing all about.

He ran and he ran, *sniff, sniff, snuff*, till his nose picked up a smell.

Aroof, arooooo, Sam sang out as he raced along a trail.

And whooping and hollering, Little Arliss always chased behind.

Arliss and Sam went hunting just about every day.

They trailed raccoons together.
They tracked down foxes together.
They hunted rabbits together.

And they treed bobcats together.
Come dark—the rascals even slept together.

Well, one day Mr. Coates got the buckboard wagon ready.

"A new family just moved in on the other side of Salt Licks," he said. "Let's go and visit them."

Little Arliss yelled, "Sam! Come here—we're going visiting!"

But his father shook his head. "Sorry, Arliss. Sam can't go."

Arliss made an angry face.

"Now listen to me, Arliss Coates," his father said. "Sam's a fine hunting dog, but he's too rascally for visiting. We're not taking him—and that's that."

That was that, all right.

They took along some hog-plum jelly that Mrs. Coates had made. They took along a jar of wild honey and a jug of fresh buttermilk. They took Arliss along, and his big brother Travis.

Then they tied Sam to the split-rail fence. And off they went in the buckboard wagon.

First Sam howled
sadly.

Then, for a while,
he sat still.

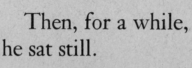

But just for a while.   Sam was too rascally;
he never could sit still for long.

Sam scrambled to his feet and started chewing
on the rawhide string.

In the back of the wagon, Arliss grumbled,

"It's not fair. Jumper came along. If a mule can come, why can't a dog?"

"Now, Arliss," his mother hushed him, "Jumper has to pull the wagon, and you know it."

The buckboard wagon bounded and jounced over rocks and ruts. They still had a long way to go.

At last they rode up to the new family's cabin.

"Welcome to Salt Licks!" Mr. Coates called out in his cheeriest voice.

"Good of you to come," the new man said. His name was Andrews. "Get right down and make yourselves at home."

Mr. Andrews and his wife had only one child—a wide-eyed girl who was Travis's age. And they didn't even have a dog.

The grownups talked together, and the girl talked to Travis. And Arliss sat by himself on the water barrel, with nobody to talk to and nothing to do.

But Arliss didn't sit there for long; he was too rascally.

Arliss wandered off.

He came to a cool stream. For a while he waded there. Then he wandered off again.

He came to a grassy slope. For a while he chased a rabbit there. Then he wandered off again.

After that he came to a steep trail.
Arliss slipped and slid halfway down the trail.

But then he tripped over a stone.   And falling,
he rolled down to the bottom.

When Arliss tried to get up, he sank back
with a groan.   He had hurt his ankle.

"I'm in a fine fix," he thought. "I can't walk. And the new family has no dog. Everybody will come out looking for me. But there's no telling how long it will be before they ever find me."

Just then, not too far away, a bobcat gave a coughing roar.

Little Arliss shivered. He surely wished that Sam had come along today.

Savage Sam, at that moment, was giving yips of joy. For he had just chewed through the rawhide string.

Soon Sam stopped yipping and started sniffing. He ran along, winding here and there, *sniff*, *sniff*, *snuff*, till his nose picked up a smell.

Aroof, arooooo, Sam sang out as he raced along the trail.

What was Sam going after? Bear? Fox? Raccoon?

No! He was trailing Arliss.

Ah-rooooo! Sam trailed Arliss all the way to the new family's cabin.

There he ran around and around, *sniff, sniff, snuff,* till he picked up the trail again.

Roof-roof, arooooo, Sam splashed across the stream, raced up the slope, and slipped and slid down the steep trail.

At the bottom, he found Arliss.

Arliss hugged him and Sam yipped and barked with joy.

After a while Mr. Coates came down the trail. Travis was with him, so was Mr. Andrews.

Mr. Coates said, "We were out looking for you, Arliss. But we had no luck till we heard Sam go by. We followed his voice, and here we are."

Mr. Andrews couldn't get over it.

He asked, "How did the dog know that Arliss was in trouble?"

"Sam knew only one thing," Mr. Coates answered as he scooped Arliss up. "And that was that Arliss went off without him. There's just no keeping that dog and boy apart."

"Papa," Arliss asked later, "will we take Savage Sam along the next time we go visiting?" "I reckon we might as well," his father said. And that was that.